POPULAR LEGENDS

By

Count Leo N. Tolstóy

Fredonia Books
Amsterdam, The Netherlands

Popular Legends

by
Leo N. Tolstoy

Translated by Leo Wiener

ISBN: 1-4101-0514-8

Reprinted from the 1904 edition

Fredonia Books
Amsterdam, The Netherlands
http://www.fredoniabooks.com

In order to make original editions of historical works available to scholars at an economical price, this facsimile of the original edition of 1904 is reproduced from the best available copy and has been digitally enhanced to improve legibility, but the text remains unaltered to retain historical authenticity.

CONTENTS

POPULAR LEGENDS

1886

POPULAR LEGENDS

———•———

HOW THE DEVIL REDEEMED THE CRUST OF BREAD

A POOR peasant went out to plough, without having had his breakfast, and took with him from home a crust of bread. The peasant turned over the plough and untied the beam, which he put under a bush; here he also placed his crust of bread, which he covered with his caftan.

The horse grew tired, and the peasant was hungry. The peasant stuck fast the plough, unhitched the horse and let it go to graze, and himself went to his caftan, to have his dinner. He raised the caftan, but the crust was not there; he searched and searched for it, and turned his caftan around and shook it, but the crust was gone. The peasant marvelled.

"This is remarkable," he thought. "I have not seen any one, and yet somebody has carried off the crust of bread."

But it was a little devil who, while the peasant had been ploughing, had carried off the crust; he sat down behind a bush to hear how the peasant would curse and scold him, the devil.

The peasant looked a bit dejected.

"Well," he said, "I shall not starve. Evidently the one who carried it off needed it. May he eat it to his health!"

3

And the peasant went to the well, drank some water, rested himself, caught the horse, hitched it up, and began once more to plough.

The little devil felt sad because he had not led the peasant into sin, and went to the chief devil to tell him about it.

He appeared before the chief devil and told him how he had carried off the peasant's crust, and how the peasant, instead of cursing, had told him to eat it to his health. The chief devil grew angry.

"If the peasant has in this business got the better of you," he said, "it is your own fault, — you did not know any better. If the peasants, and the women, after them, take such a notion, we shall have a hard time of it. This matter cannot be left in such a shape. Go," he said, "once more to the peasant, and earn the crust. If in three years you do not get the better of the peasant, I will bathe you in holy water."

The little devil was frightened. He ran down upon the earth, and began to think how he might redeem his guilt. He thought and thought, and finally thought it out. He turned into a good man, and hired himself out as a labourer to the peasant. He taught the peasant in a dry year to sow in a swamp. The peasant listened to his hired hand and sowed the grain in the swamp. The other peasants had all their grain burned up by the sun, but the poor peasant's corn grew thick, tall, and with full ears. The peasant had enough to eat until the next crop, and much corn was left. In the summer the hired hand taught the peasant to sow on the uplands. It turned out to be a rainy summer. The corn of the other peasants fell down and rotted and made no ears, but this peasant's corn on the uplands was heavy with ears. The peasant had now even more corn left, and he did not know what to do with it.

The hired hand taught the peasant to mash the grain

and brew liquor. The peasant brewed some liquor, and began to drink himself and to give it to others. The little devil came to his chief, and began to boast that he had earned the crust. The chief devil went to look for himself.

He came to the peasant, and saw that the peasant had invited some rich men, to treat them to liquor. The hostess was carrying the liquor around to the guests. As she walked around, her foot caught in the table, and she spilled a glass. The peasant grew angry, and scolded his wife.

"Devil's fool," he said. "Is this slops that you, with your clumsy hands, spill such precious liquor on the ground?"

The little devil nudged his chief.

"Watch him!" he said. "Now he will regret his crust."

The host scolded his wife, and began himself to carry the liquor around. A poor peasant, who had not been invited, came back from his work. He greeted the company and sat down, watching the people drink the liquor; as he was tired he wanted to have a drink himself. He sat and sat, and swallowed his spittle, — but the host did not offer him any; he only muttered:

"Where will a man get enough liquor for the whole lot of you?"

This, too, pleased the chief devil; but the little devil boasted:

"Wait, it will be worse than that."

The rich peasants had a glass, and so had the host. They began to flatter one another and to praise one another, and to speak oily, deceptive words. The chief devil listened to that, too, and was glad of it.

"If this drink will make them so foxy, and they will deceive one another," he said, "they will be in our hands."

" Wait," said the little devil, " and see what is coming: let them drink another glass. Now they wag their tails to one another, like foxes, and want to deceive one another, but look, they will soon be like fierce wolves."

The peasants had another glass, and their words became louder and coarser. Instead of oily speeches, they began to curse and to get angry with one another, and they fell to, and mauled one another's noses. The host, too, took a hand in the fight. And he was also beaten.

The chief devil saw this, too, and was glad.

" This," he said, " is nice."

But the little devil said:

" Wait, it will be better yet! Let them have a third glass. Now they are like mad wolves, but let them have a third glass, and they will become like swine."

The peasants had a third glass. They went completely to pieces. They muttered and yelled, they did not know themselves what, and paid no attention to one another. They began to scatter, some going away by themselves, and some by twos and threes; they all fell down and wallowed in the street. The host went out to see them off, and he fell with his nose in the gutter, and he became all soiled and lay there like a pig, grunting.

This pleased the chief devil even more.

" Well," he said, " you have invented a fine drink, and you have earned the crust. Tell me how you made this drink. It cannot be otherwise than that you have first let into it some fox blood, — and this made the peasant as sly as a fox. And then you let in some wolf blood, — and this made him as fierce as a wolf. And finally you poured in some pig blood, and this made him a pig."

" No," said the little devil, " that was not the way I did. All I did was to let him have more corn than he needed. That beast blood has always lived in him, but it has no chance so long as he gets barely enough corn. At that time he was not sorry even for the last crust, but when he began to have a surplus from his corn, he began to think of how he might have his fun from it. And I taught him the fun of drinking liquor. And when he began to brew God's gift into liquor for his fun, there arose in him his fox, wolf, and pig blood. Let him now drink liquor, and he will always be a beast."

The chief praised the little devil, forgave him for the crust of bread, and made him a captain.

THE REPENTANT SINNER

And he said unto Jesus, Lord, remember me when thou comest into thy kingdom.

And Jesus said unto him, Verily I say unto thee, To-day shalt thou be with me in paradise. (Luke xxiii. 42, 43.)

THERE was a man who had lived seventy years in the world, and had passed all his life in sins. And he grew sick, and did not repent. And when his time came to die, he wept in the last hour, and said:

O Lord! Forgive me as Thou forgavest the thief on the cross.

No sooner had he said this than his soul left him.

And the soul of the sinner loved God, and believed in His goodness, and came to the gate of heaven. And the sinner knocked at the door, and begged to be let in. And he heard a voice behind the door:

"What man is this that is knocking at the door of heaven? And what deeds has this man done in his life?"

And the voice of the arraigner answered, and counted out all the sinful deeds of this man, and did not mention a single good deed.

And a voice answered behind the door:

"Sinners cannot enter into the kingdom of heaven. Go hence."

And the man said:

"Lord, I hear thy voice, but do not see thy face, and do not know thy name."

And the voice answered:

"I am Peter the apostle."

And the sinner said:

"Have pity on me, Peter the apostle. Remember human weakness and God's love. Wert thou not Christ's disciple, and heardst thou not His teaching from His very lips, and sawest thou not the examples of His life? Remember, when He was dejected and troubled in spirit, and commanded thee three times not to sleep, but to pray, thou didst sleep, because thy eyes were heavy, and three times He found thee sleeping. Even so it is with me. And remember again, how thou didst promise Him not to renounce Him until His death, and how thou didst deny Him three times, when they took Him before Caiaphas. Even so it is with me. And remember again, how the cock crew, and thou didst go out and weep bitterly. Even so it is with me. Thou canst not keep me out."

And the voice behind the door of heaven grew silent.

And the sinner stood awhile, and began once more to knock at the door, and to beg to be admitted into the kingdom of heaven.

And another voice was heard behind the door, saying:

"Who is this man, and how did he live in the world?"

And the voice of the arraigner answered, again repeating all the evil deeds of the sinner, and did not mention any good deeds whatsoever.

And the voice behind the door answered:

"Go hence, for such sinners cannot live with us in heaven."

And the sinner said:

"Lord, I hear thy voice, but do not see thy face, and do not know thy name."

And the voice said to him:

"I am David, the king and prophet."

But the sinner did not despair. He did not go away from the door of heaven, but said:

"Have mercy on me, King David, and remember human weakness and God's love. God loved thee and exalted thee above men. Thou hadst everything, a kingdom, and glory, and riches, and wives, and children, but when thou sawest from thy roof the wife of a poor man, sin entered thee, and thou tookest the wife of Uriah, and slewest him with the sword of the Ammonites. Thou, a rich man, tookest the last sheep away from a poor man, and then didst destroy him. Even so did I. Then remember how thou repentedst, saying, 'I confess my guilt, and am contrite on account of my sin.' Even so did I. Thou canst not keep me out."

And the voice behind the door grew silent.

And having tarried awhile, the sinner began to knock once more and to beg to be let into the kingdom of heaven. And a third voice was heard, saying:

"Who is this man? And how did he live in the world?"

And the voice of the arraigner answered, for the third time recounting the evil deeds of the man, and did not mention any good deeds.

And a voice behind the door answered:

"Go hence. Sinners cannot enter into the kingdom of heaven."

And the sinner answered:

"I hear thy voice, but do not see thy face, and do not know thy name."

And the voice replied:

"I am John the Divine, the beloved disciple of Christ."

And the sinner rejoiced and said:

"Now I cannot be kept out. Peter and David will let me in, because they know human weakness and God's love; but thou wilt let me in, because there is much love in thee. Didst thou, John the Divine, not write in thy book that God is love, and that he who does not love does not know God? Didst thou not in thy old age say this word to men: 'Brethren, love one another'? How, then, canst thou hate me and drive me away? Either thou shalt renounce what thou didst say, or thou shalt love me and let me enter into the kingdom of God."

And the gates of heaven opened, and John embraced the repentant sinner, and let him enter into the kingdom of God.

THE KERNEL OF THE SIZE OF A HEN'S EGG

ONE day some children found in a ravine something that looked like a hen's egg with a parting in the middle and resembling a kernel. A traveller saw this thing in the children's hands, and he bought it from them for a nickel, and took it to town, and sold it to the king as a rarity.

The king called the wise men and commanded them to find out what the thing was, whether an egg or a kernel. The wise men thought and thought, but could give no answer. The thing was lying on the window-sill, and a hen flew in and picked at it, until it picked a hole in it: then all saw that it was a kernel. The wise men went to the king and told the king that it was a rye kernel.

The king was surprised. He commanded the wise men to find out where and when this kernel had grown. The wise men thought and thought, and hunted through books, and could not find out. In our books nothing is written about it; it was necessary to ask the peasants whether one of the old men had not heard when and where such a kernel had been sowed.

The king commanded that a very old peasant be brought into his presence. They found such a man, and brought him to the king. There arrived a green-skinned, toothless old man, and he barely could walk with his two crutches.

The king showed him the kernel; but the old man could not see well. He half looked at it, and half felt it with his hands.

The king began to ask him : "Do you not know, grandfather, where such a kernel was raised ? Have you not raised such grain ? Or did you not some day during your life buy such a seed ? "

The old man was deaf, and he barely heard what the king was saying, and barely made it out. Then the old man began to speak :

" No, I have not raised such grain in my field, and have never reaped such, nor have I bought such. Whenever I bought grain, it was always small. But I must ask my father," he said, " perhaps he has heard of such grain."

The king sent for the old man's father, and commanded that he be brought into his presence. They found the old man's father, and brought him to the king. The old man came on one crutch. The king showed him the kernel. The old man could see with his eyes. He took a good look at it. The king began to ask him :

" Do you not know, old man, where such a kernel was grown ? Have you never raised such in your own field ? Or have you ever bought such kernels in your life ? "

Though the old man was rather hard of hearing, he heard better than his son.

" No," he said, " I have never sowed such seed in my field, and have never reaped such. Nor have I ever bought such, as in my day money was not yet in existence. We all lived on our own grain, and in case of need shared with our neighbours. I do not know where such a kernel was grown. Though our grain used to be larger and more millable than what it is now, I never saw such. I used to hear my father say that in his day the grain was larger and more millable than ours. You will have to ask him."

The king sent for his father. They found the man, and he was brought to the king. The old man walked into the king's room without any crutches. He walked lightly, — his eyes were bright, and he could hear well, and talked distinctly. The king showed the kernel to the old man. The old man looked at it, and turned it around.

"It is now long since I last saw such grain."

The old man bit off a piece of the kernel, and chewed it.

"It is that," he said.

"Tell me, grandfather, when and where such a kernel was raised? Did you never sow such in your own field? Or did you ever buy it of people in your lifetime?"

And the old man said:

"In my day such grain was raised everywhere. With such corn I fed myself and other people. Such grain I sowed, and reaped, and threshed."

And the king asked:

"Tell me, grandfather, did you buy such grain, or did you sow it in your own field?"

The old man smiled.

"In my day," he said, "no one ever thought of such a sin as selling or buying grain. We did not know anything about money. Everybody had enough corn of his own."

And the king asked:

"Then tell me, grandfather, where you sowed such corn, and where your field was?"

And the old man said:

"My field was God's earth. Wherever I ploughed, there was the field. The land was free. They did not call it one's own land. People called nothing but their labour their own."

"Tell me, then," said the king, "two more things: one is, why formerly you used to grow such grain, and now such grain does not grow. The other is, why your grandson walked with two crutches, while your son came with one, and you walk entirely at your ease: your eyes are bright, your teeth strong, and your speech clear and pleasing. Grandfather, how did these two things happen?"

And the old man said :

" These things are so because people have stopped living by their own labour, and are having an eye to other people's labour. They did not live that way of old ; of old they lived in godly fashion, — they owned what was their own, and did not profit by what belonged to others."

HOW MUCH LAND A MAN NEEDS

I.

THE elder sister came with her younger sister to the country. The elder was married to a merchant in the city, and the younger to a peasant in the village. The sisters were drinking tea, and talking. The elder began to boast, — to praise her city life, — telling how comfortably and how cleanly they lived in the city, how she dressed up the children, what savoury food and drink she had, and how she went to picnics and entertainments and theatres.

The younger sister felt offended, and began to speak disparagingly of the merchant life, and to extol the life of the peasants.

"I would not exchange my life for yours," she said. "It is true, we live uncleanly, but we do not know what fear is. You live more cleanly, but you either make a lot of money, or you lose it all. And the proverb says, 'Gain loves more.' And it happens that to-day you are rich, and to-morrow you lie in the gutter. But our peasant business is surer; a peasant's life is slim, but long; we are not rich, but have enough to eat."

The elder sister said:

"Yes, enough to eat, but with pigs and calves! You aren't dressed up, and have no manners. No matter how much your man may work, you live in manure, and so you will die, leaving nothing to your children."

"What of it?" said the younger. "Such is our business. But we are independent, and do not bow to any

16

one, and fear no one. But you live in the cities among temptations: to-day it is all right, and to-morrow the unclean one will turn up and tempt your man either with cards, or with wine, or with some damsel. And then all will go to the winds. Do not such things happen ? "

Pakhóm, her husband, lying on the oven, heard the women's prattle.

" That is the gospel truth," he said. " Our kind have been turning over mother earth ever since our childhood, and so foolishness has no time to enter into our heads. There is just this trouble, — we have not enough land ! If I had as much land as I want, I would not be afraid of the devil himself."

The women drank their tea, prattled awhile about dresses, put away the dishes and went to sleep.

But the devil had been sitting behind the oven, and listening to all they said. He was glad to hear the peasant woman make her husband boast that if he had enough land, the devil would not take him.

" Very well," he thought, " we shall have a tussle: I will give you lots of land. I will overcome you by means of the land."

II.

By the side of the peasants there lived a small proprietress. She had 120 desyatínas of land. So far she had lived in peace with the peasants, and had offended no one; but an ex-soldier hired out to her as a steward, and he began to wear the peasants out with fines. No matter how careful Pakhóm was, either his horse would run into the oats, or a cow would lose her way in the garden, or the calves would stray into the meadow, — for everything he had to pay a fine.

Pakhóm paid the fines, and scolded and beat his home people. And so Pakhóm suffered many an insult from that steward during the summer, and was glad when they began to stable the cattle, — though he was sorry they could not graze, he at least had no more fear.

In the winter the rumour was spread that the proprietress was going to sell her land, and that an innkeeper on the highway was trying to buy it. When the peasants heard this, they groaned.

" Well," they thought, " if the innkeeper gets the land, he will wear us out with fines even worse than the proprietress. We cannot live without this land, — we live all around it."

The peasants went to the proprietress and began to ask her not to sell it to the innkeeper, but to let them have it. They promised they would pay more for it. The lady consented. The peasants were thinking of buying the land in common : they met once and twice to discuss the matter, but it did not work. The evil one brought discord among them, and they could not agree. Finally the peasants agreed to buy the land in lots, as much as each could afford to buy. The lady agreed even to this. Pakhóm heard that a neighbour of his had bought twenty desyatínas, and that she had given him time for half the sum. Pakhóm felt jealous : " They will buy up all the land," he thought, " and I shall be left with nothing." He began to take counsel with his wife.

" People are buying the land," he said, " and we, too, ought to buy a few desyatínas of it. We cannot get along now, for the steward has ruined me with the fines."

They considered how they might buy it. They had one hundred roubles put away, and they sold a colt, and half of the bees, and hired out their son as a labourer, and borrowed some from a relative, and thus got together half the sum.

Pakhóm took the money, picked out fifteen desyatínas with a little grove, and went to the lady to strike a bargain. He bought the fifteen desyatínas, clinched the bargain, and paid an earnest. They drove to the city and made out a deed, and he paid half the sum and promised to pay the rest in two years.

Thus Pakhóm became possessed of land. He borrowed seed and sowed in the purchased land, and it produced a good crop. In one year he paid his debt to the lady and to his relative. And so Pakhóm became a proprietor: he ploughed and sowed in his own land, mowed on his own land, cut poles off his own land, and pastured his cattle on his own land. Pakhóm took great delight in ploughing the land which belonged to him for all time, and in going out to look at the sprouting corn and at the meadows. It seemed to him as though the grass grew and the flowers bloomed quite differently on them. He had crossed this land many a time before, and it had been just land to him; but now it was something quite different.

III.

Thus Pakhóm lived, enjoying himself. All would have been well, but the peasants began to trespass on Pakhóm's fields and meadows. He begged them in kindness, but they paid no attention to him: now the shepherds let the cows get into his meadows, and now the horses would leave their right pastures and run into his corn. Pakhóm drove them off, and forgave the peasants, and did not sue them; finally he got tired of it, and began to complain in the township office. He knew that the peasants were not doing it from malice, but because they were crowded, but he thought: "I cannot let them off, for they will ruin all my fields. I must teach them a lesson."

He taught them one or two lessons in court, and this and that man were fined. His neighbours began to have a grudge against him, and occasionally trespassed on his land intentionally. Some one stole in the night into his grove and cut down ten lindens for bast. As Pakhóm passed by the grove, he noticed something white there. He drove up to the spot, and found the barked lindens on the ground, and the stumps standing. "If he had just cut off the outer bushes and left the main tree standing! But no, the rascal has cut them all down." Pakhóm grew angry.

"Oh," he thought, "if I could just find out who did it; I would get my revenge on him." He thought and thought who it could be; "It cannot be any one but Sémka."

He went into Sémka's yard to look for them, but found there nothing, and they only had a quarrel. Pakhóm became even more convinced that it was Sémka. He entered a complaint. They were summoned to court. They tried and tried the case, and discharged the peasant, for there was no evidence. Pakhóm grew angrier than ever, and he scolded the elder and the judges.

"You are in with the thieves," he said. "If you yourselves lived honestly, you would not let the thieves go free."

Pakhóm quarrelled with the judges and with his neighbours. They began to threaten to set fire to his house. Pakhóm lived more comfortably on his land, but less comfortably in the Commune.

Just then they began to spread a rumour that people were going to new places. And Pakhóm thought:

"I have no reason for leaving my own land; but if some of our men would go there, there would be more room here. I would take up their land and would attach it to my own. I should live more comfortably than I do now, for now I am crowded!"

Pakhóm was sitting at home one day, when a transient peasant stepped in. They invited the peasant to stay overnight, and gave him to eat, and talked with him, asking him whence God had brought him. The peasant said that he had come from farther down, from beyond

the Vólga, where he had been working. One word led to
another, and he told them how people were rushing
to settle down there. He told them that men from his
village had settled there, joining the Commune, and receiving ten desyatínas to each soul. The land was such,
he said, that they planted rye which grew to be higher
than a horse, and so thick that about five handfuls made
a sheaf. There was one peasant, he said, who had been
poor, and had come with nothing but his hands, and now
had six horses and two cows.

This excited Pakhóm. He thought:

" Why suffer here where it is crowded, if it is possible
to live better ? I will sell the land and the farm; there
I will start a new farm with this money, and will provide
myself with everything. Here, where it is crowded, it is
just a shame to stay. But I must first find it all out
myself."

He got ready in the summer, and started out. Down
to Samára he went on a steamer, then he made four hundred versts on foot. He reached the place. It was all
as he had been told: the peasants were living freely, with
ten desyatínas of land to each soul, and glad to receive
people into their Communes. And if a man had money,
he could, in addition to the grant, buy in perpetual pos-
session the very best land at three roubles : he could get
all the land he wanted.

Pakhóm found out everything he wanted. He returned
home in the fall, and began to sell everything. He sold
his land at a profit, and his farm, and all his cattle ; he
gave up his membership in the Commune, and waited for
spring, and went with his whole family to the new places.

IV.

Pakhóm arrived with his family in the new places,
where he joined the Commune of a large village. He

treated the old men and got all the papers made out. They received Pakhóm, and apportioned to him for his five souls fifty desyatínas in various fields, not counting the common pasture.

Pakhóm built a hut and bought cattle. He had now three times as much land as before, and it was fruitful land. He began to live ten times as well as before. He had all the fields and meadows he wanted. He could keep as many cattle as he pleased.

At first, while he was building and getting things into shape, everything looked nice to Pakhóm; but when he got used to it, he began once more to feel crowded. The first year Pakhóm sowed wheat on the grant land, and he had a good crop. He got it into his head to sow wheat, but the grant land was not enough for him, and what there was of it was no good. There they were sowing wheat on prairie land. They sowed it in for two years, and then let it lie fallow, to grow up again with prairie grass. There were many who wanted to have such land, so that there was not enough land to go around. And there were quarrels about it: those who were better off wanted to sow on it themselves, and the poor people gave it to the merchants for the taxes. Pakhóm wanted to sow as much as possible. He went the next year to a merchant, and bought land for the period of a year. He went the next year to the merchant, and again bought land for a year. He sowed more wheat, and he had a good crop, only it was far away from the village, — he had to haul the wheat fifteen versts. He saw the merchant peasants of the district living in their estates, and getting rich.

"It would be nice," thought Pakhóm, "if I myself bought land in perpetuity, and established an estate for myself. Everything would be adjoining me."

And Pakhóm began to think how he might buy land in perpetuity.

Thus Pakhóm lived for three years. He rented land, and sowed wheat. The years were good, and the wheat grew well, and he had some money laid by. He could live and live, but it appeared tiresome to Pakhóm to buy new land from people each year, and to have to fuss about the land: where there was any good land the peasants would swoop down on it and take it all up, and unless he was quick in getting it, he would not have any land to sow in. And in the third year he rented with a merchant a pasture on shares, and they ploughed it all up, but the peasants from whom they rented it went to court about it, and all their work was lost. "If it were all my land," he thought, "I should not bow to any one, and there would be no worry."

Pakhóm began to inquire where he could buy land in perpetuity, and he found a peasant who would sell. The peasant had bought five hundred desyatínas, but he had lost money, and now wanted to sell the land cheap. Pakhóm began to bargain with him. He bargained and bargained, and finally got it for fifteen hundred roubles, half of it on time. They had almost settled the matter, when a transient merchant stopped at his farm to get something to eat. They drank tea, and started to talk. The merchant told him that he had come from the far-off country of the Bashkirs. There, he said, he had bought about five thousand desyatínas from the Bashkirs, and for this he had to pay only one thousand roubles. Pakhóm began to question him. The merchant told him all about it.

"All I had to do," he said, "was to gain over the old men. I gave in presents about one hundred roubles' worth of cloaks and rugs, and a caddy of tea, and filled up with wine those who would drink. I gave twenty kopeks per desyatína." He showed the deed. "The land," he said, "lies along a river, and it is all a prairie."

Pakhóm began to question him all about it.

"You can't walk around the land in a year," he said,
"and it all belongs to the Bashkirs. And the people
have no sense, just like sheep. You can get it almost
for nothing."

"Well," thought Pakhóm, "why do I want to buy
five hundred desyatínas for one thousand roubles, and
take a debt on my neck? There I can get rich for one
thousand roubles."

V.

Pakhóm inquired how to get there, and as soon as he
saw the merchant off he got ready to go. He left his
house to his wife, and took his hired help, and went with
him. They travelled to the city, bought a caddy of tea,
presents, and wine, just as the merchant had said. They
travelled and travelled, until they had five hundred versts
behind them. On the seventh day they came to the
Bashkir roaming-grounds. Everything was as the merchant had said. They all live in the steppe, above the
river, in felt tents. They themselves neither plough
nor eat bread, but the cattle and horses run in droves in
the steppe. Back of the tents the colts are tied, and
twice a day they drive the mares there, and milk them,
and make kumys of the milk. The women churn the
kumys and make cheese, and all the men do is to drink
kumys and tea, eat mutton, and play a pipe. They look
sleek and merry, and they celebrate the whole summer.
The people are all ignorant, and know no Russian, but
they are kind.

As soon as they saw Pakhóm, they came out of their
tents, and surrounded the guest. There was an interpreter there. Pakhóm told him that he had come to see
about some land. The Bashkirs were happy, and they
took Pakhóm by his arms, and led him to a nice tent,
seated him on rugs, placed down pillows under him, sat
around him in a circle, and began to treat him to tea and

to kumys. They killed a sheep, and filled him with mutton. Pakhóm fetched the presents from the tarantás, and began to distribute them to the Bashkirs. Pakhóm gave the presents to the Bashkirs, and distributed the tea among them. The Bashkirs were happy. They prattled among themselves, and then told the interpreter to translate.

"They command me to tell you," said the interpreter, "that they like you, and that it is our custom to give our guests every pleasure, and to return presents. You have given us presents; now tell us what you like us to give you of our things."

"What I like," said Pakhóm, "most of all, here, is your land. Where I live," he said, "the land is crowded and worn out by ploughing, but you have much and good land. I have never seen such before."

The interpreter translated. The Bashkirs talked among themselves. Pakhóm did not understand what they were saying, but he saw that they were merry, shouting and laughing. Then they grew silent, and looked at Pakhóm, but the interpreter said:

"They command me to tell you that for the good which you have done them they are glad to give you as much land as you want. You have just to point to it, and it is yours."

Then they talked again, and disputed among themselves. Pakhóm asked what they were disputing, and the interpreter said:

"Some say that they must ask the elder about the land, and that they cannot do it without him. But others say that they can do it without him."

VI.

The Bashkirs went on disputing, when suddenly a man in a fox cap came in. They all grew silent and got up, and the interpreter said:

"This is their elder."

Pakhóm immediately took out the best cloak and five pounds of tea, and took this to the elder. The elder received the presents, and sat down in the place of honour. The Bashkirs began at once to talk to him. The elder listened and listened to them, and shook his head to them, for them to keep quiet. Then he began to speak in Russian to Pakhóm.

"Well, you may have it," he said. "Take it wherever you like. There is a great deal of land here."

"How can I take as much as I want?" thought Pakhóm. "I must get some statement, or else they will say that it is mine, and then they will take it away from me."

"Thank you," he said, "for your kind words. You have a great deal of land, but I want only a small part of it. How shall I know which is mine? I must measure it off, and get a statement of some kind. For God disposes of life and of death. You good people give it to me, but your children may come and take it away."

"You are right," said the elder, "we shall give you a statement."

Then Pakhóm said:

"I have heard that a merchant came to see you. You made him a present of some land and gave him a deed: I ought to get one myself."

The elder understood it all.

"That is all possible," he said. "We have a scribe, and we will go to town, and affix our seals."

"And what will the price be?" asked Pakhóm.

"We have but one price: one thousand roubles a day."

Pakhóm did not understand him.

"What kind of a measure is a day? How many desyatínas are there in it?"

"We cannot figure it out," he said. "We sell by the

day; as much as you can walk over in one day is yours, and a day's price is one thousand roubles."

Pakhóm was surprised.

" But in one day you can walk around a great deal of land," he said.

The elder laughed.

" It is all yours," he said. " But there is just one condition: if you do not come back in one day to the place from which you start, your money is lost."

" But how can I mark off what I walk over?" asked Pakhóm.

" We shall stand on the spot which you will choose, and you will start on the circuit: take with you a spade, and wherever necessary, in the corners, dig a hole, and pile up some turf, and we shall later make a furrow with a plough from hole to hole. Make any circuit you please, but by sundown you must come back to the spot from which you have started. Whatever ground you cover is yours."

Pakhóm was happy. They decided to go out early in the morning. They talked awhile, drank more kumys, ate some mutton, and had tea again; it was getting dark. They bedded Pakhóm on feather beds, and then the Bashkirs went away. They promised to meet him at daybreak, and to go out to the spot before the sun was up.

VII.

Pakhóm lay down on the feather bed and could not sleep: he was thinking all the time of the land.

" I will slice off a mighty tract," he thought. " I can walk about fifty versts in one day. The day is long now; in fifty versts there will be a lot of land. The worst I will sell, or let to the peasants, and the best I will keep, and will settle on myself. I will buy me two ox-teams and will hire two more hands; I will plough up about fifty desyatínas, and on the rest I will let the cattle roam."

Pakhóm could not fall asleep all night. It was only before daybreak that he forgot himself. The moment he became unconscious, he had a dream. He saw himself lying in the same tent, and some one on the outside was roaring with laughter. He wanted to see who was laughing there, and he thought he went out of the tent, and saw the same Bashkir sitting before the tent, holding his belly with both his hands and swaying in his laughter. He went up to him and said: "What are you laughing about?" And it seemed to him that it was not the Bashkir, but the merchant who had stopped at his house and had told him all about the land. And he asked the merchant: "How long have you been here?" But it was no longer the merchant; it was the peasant that long ago had come from the lower country. And Pakhóm saw that it was not the peasant, but the devil himself with horns and hoofs: he was sitting, and laughing, and before him lay a man, in his bare feet, and in a shirt and trousers. And Pakhóm took a closer look to see who the man was. And he saw that it was a dead man, — himself. Pakhóm was frightened, and awoke. "A man will dream anything," he said, as he awoke. He looked around through the open door, and day was breaking, and it was getting light.

"I must wake the people now," he thought, "it is time to start."

Pakhóm got up, woke his labourer in the tarantás, ordered him to hitch up, and went himself to wake the Bashkirs.

"It is time to go out to lay off the land," he said.

The Bashkirs got up, and gathered together, and the elder arrived. The Bashkirs began again to drink kumys and wanted to treat Pakhóm to tea, but he would not wait so long.

"If we are to go, let us go," he said.   "It is time."

VIII.

The Bashkirs came together, and some went on horse-back, and others in tarantáses, and they started. Pakhóm went with his labourer in his little tarantás, taking a spade with them. They arrived in the steppe just as it was dawning. They rode up a mound, called "shikhan" in the Bashkir language. They got out of their tarantáses and dismounted from their horses, and gathered in a circle. The elder walked over to Pakhóm, and pointed with his hand.

"Everything you see," he said, "is ours. Choose whatever you please."

Pakhóm's eyes were burning: it was all prairie land, as smooth as the palm of the hand and as black as the poppy, and wherever there was a hollow there were different kinds of grass, breast-high.

The elder took off his fox cap and put it on the ground.

"This will be the goal," he said. "From here you will start, and here you will come back. Whatever you circle about will be yours."

Pakhóm took out the money, put it on the cap, and pulled off his caftan, and so was left in his sleeveless coat. He pulled his girdle tighter over his belly, drew up his trousers, put a wallet with bread in his bosom, tied a can of water to his belt, pulled up his boot-legs, took the spade from his labourer, and got ready to go. He thought for awhile in what direction to start, — it was nice everywhere. He thought: "It makes no difference. I will go eastward." He turned his face toward the sun, stretched himself, and waited for the sun to peep out. He thought: "I must not waste time in vain. It is easier to walk while it is fresh." The moment the sun just glistened over the edge, Pakhóm threw the spade over his shoulder and started over the steppe.

Pakhóm walked neither leisurely, nor fast. He walked about a verst; he stopped, dug a hole, and put some turf in a heap, so as to make the sign clearer. He went on. He was getting limbered up, and he increased his step. After walking a distance, he dug another hole.

Pakhóm looked around. The shikhan could easily be seen in the sunshine, and the people were standing there, and the tires on the wheels of the tarantáses glistened. Pakhóm guessed that he had walked five versts. He was getting warm, so he took off his coat, threw it over his shoulder, and marched on. It grew warm. He looked at the sun. It was time to think of breakfast.

"I have walked the distance of a ploughing," thought Pakhóm, "and there are four of them in a day, — it is too early yet to turn. I must just take off my boots."

He sat down, pulled off his boots, stuck them in his girdle, and started off again. It was easy to walk now. He thought: "I will walk another five versts, then I will turn to the left. The land is so fine, it is a pity to leave it out." The farther he went, the nicer it was. He went straight ahead. He turned back to look: the shikhan was barely visible, and the people looked like black ants, and something could barely be seen glistening in the sun.

"Well," thought Pakhóm, "I have walked enough in this direction. I must turn in. I am hot, too: I must take a drink."

He stopped, dug a large hole, piled up the turf, untied the can, took a drink, and bent sharply to the left. He walked on and on, and the grass was high, and he felt hot.

Pakhóm was beginning to grow tired; he looked at the sun, and saw that it was exactly noon.

"Well," he thought, "I must take a rest."

Pakhóm stopped and sat down. He ate a piece of bread and drank some water, but did not lie down: he

was afraid he might fall asleep. After sitting awhile
he started off again. At first the walking was easy. The
lunch gave him new strength. It grew very hot, and
he felt sleepy; but he kept walking, thinking that he
would have to suffer but a little while, and would have to
live long.

He walked quite a distance in this direction. He was
on the point of turning, when, behold, he came upon a
wet hollow; it was a pity to lose this. He thought
that flax would do well there. He walked on straight.
He took in the hollow, then dug a hole beyond it, and
turned around the second corner. Pakhóm looked back
at the shikhan; it was mist-covered from the heat, quiv-
ering in the air, and through the haze he could barely see
the people.

"Well," thought Pakhóm, "I have taken two long
sides. I must make this one shorter."

He started on his third side, and began to increase his
speed. He looked at the sun, and it was already near
the middle of the afternoon, but he had made only two
versts on the third side. To the goal it was still fifteen
versts.

"Yes," he thought, "though it is going to be a crooked
estate, I must walk in a straight line. I must not take in
too much, — as it is I have a great deal."

Pakhóm quickly dug a hole, and turned straight toward
the shikhan.

IX.

Pakhóm walked straight toward the shikhan, and it
was getting hard. He was thirsty, and he had cut and
hurt his feet, and he began to totter. He wanted to rest,
but he could not, for he would not get back by sundown.
The sun did not wait, and kept going down and down.

"Oh," he said, "I hope I have not made a mistake and
taken in too much. What if I do not get back in time?"

He looked ahead of him at the shikhan and up at the sun : it was still far to the shikhan, and the sun was not far from the horizon.

Pakhóm walked, and it was hard for him, but he kept increasing his gait. He walked and walked, and it was far still, so he began to trot. He threw away his coat, his boots, and the can ; he threw away his cap, but held on to the spade, to lean on it.

" Oh," he thought, " I have made a mistake and have ruined the whole affair. I shall not get back before sun-down."

And terror took his breath away. He ran, and his shirt and trousers stuck to his body from perspiration, and his mouth was dry. In his breast it was as though bellows were being pumped, and in his heart there was a hammering, and his legs gave way under him. Pakhóm felt badly : he was afraid he might die from too much straining.

He was afraid he might die, but he did not dare to stop.

" I have run so much," he thought, " so how can I stop now ? They will only call me a fool."

He ran and ran, and was getting near, and could hear the Bashkirs screaming and shouting to him, but their noise made him still more excited. He ran with all his might, and the sun was getting near the edge : it was lost in the mist, and looked as red as blood. It was just beginning to go down. The sun was nearly gone, but it was no longer far to the goal. He saw the people waving their hands at him from the shikhan, and encouraging him. He saw the fox cap on the ground and the money on top of it ; and he saw the elder sitting on the ground, holding his hands over his belly. And Pakhóm recalled his dream.

" There is a lot of land," he thought, " but will God grant me to live on it ? Oh, I have ruined myself," he thought. " I shall not reach the spot."

Pakhóm looked at the sun, and it was down to the ground, — a part of it was down, and only an arch was standing out from the horizon. Pakhóm made a last effort and bent forward with his whole body : his legs hardly moved fast enough to keep him from falling. He ran up to the shikhan, when suddenly it grew dark. He looked around, and the sun was down. He groaned.

"My labour is lost," he thought.

He wanted to stop, but he heard the Bashkirs shouting to him, and then he recalled that here below it seemed to him that the sun was down, but that on the shikhan it was not yet down. Pakhóm made a last effort, and ran up the shikhan. On the shikhan it was still light. He ran up, and saw the cap. In front of the cap sat the elder, laughing and holding his hands on his belly. Pakhóm recalled the dream. He groaned, and his legs gave way, and he fell forward, and his hands touched the cap.

"You are a fine fellow!" cried the elder. "You have come into a lot of land."

Pakhóm's labourer ran up, wishing to raise him, but blood was flowing from his mouth, and he was dead.

The Bashkirs clicked their tongues, pitying him.

The labourer picked up the spade, and dug a grave for Pakhóm, as much as he measured from his feet to his head. — three arshíns. — and buried him in it.

THE GODSON

Ye have heard that it hath been said, An eye for an eye,
and a tooth for a tooth : but I say unto you, That ye resist
not evil (Matt. v. 38, 39).
Vengeance is mine ; I will repay (Rom. xii. 19).

I.

A SON was born to a poor peasant. The peasant was
delighted, and he went to his neighbour to call a godfather. The neighbour refused, — what pleasure is there
in being godfather to a poor peasant's child ? The poor
peasant went to another neighbour, and he, too, refused.

He went through the whole village, but no one would
be godfather. The peasant went to another village. On
his way he met a man and the man stopped him.

" Good morning," he said, " whither does God carry you,
man ? "

" The Lord has given me a child," said the peasant, " in
childhood a care, in old age a consolation, and after death
for my soul's remembrance ; but as I am poor, no one in
our village wants to be godfather. I am on my way to
look for a godfather."

And the stranger said :

" Take me for a godfather."

The peasant was happy, thanked the stranger, and
said :

" And whom shall I call in as a godmother ? "

" Call a merchant's daughter," said the stranger. " Go
into the town : on the square there is a stone house with

34

shops; at the entrance into the house ask the merchant to let his daughter go as a godmother."

The peasant hesitated.

"How can I," he said, "oh, godfather, go to the rich merchant? He will hold me in contempt, and will not let his daughter go."

"That is not your grief. Go and ask him. Be prepared to-morrow morning, — I will come to be sponsor."

The poor peasant returned home, and he went to town to see the merchant. He put up the horse in the yard, when the merchant himself came out.

"What do you want?" he asked.

"It is like this, Mr. Merchant. The Lord has given me a child, in childhood a care, in old age a consolation, and after death for my soul's remembrance. Please, let your daughter be his godmother."

"When will the christening be?"

"To-morrow morning."

"Very well, God be with you. She will come to-morrow to mass."

On the next day the godmother came, and so did the godfather, and the child was christened. The moment the christening was over, the godfather went away, and no one found out who he was, or ever saw him again.

II.

The child began to grow to his parents' joy: he was strong, and willing to work, and clever, and well-behaved. The boy was ten years old, when his parents had him taught to read. What it takes others five years to learn, the boy learned in one, and there was nothing else they could teach him.

Easter week came. The boy went down to see his godmother, to exchange the Easter greeting with her. When he returned home, he asked:

"Father and mother, where does my godfather live ? I should like to exchange the Easter greeting with him."

And the father said to him :

"We do not know, beloved son, where your godfather lives. We ourselves feel sorry for it. We have not seen him since he christened you. We have not heard of him, and we do not know where he lives, or whether he is alive."

The boy bowed to his father and to his mother :

"Father and mother," he said, "let me go to find him. I want to find him, — to exchange the Easter greeting with him."

The parents let him go, and he went to find his godfather.

III.

The boy left the house, and travelled on the highway. After walking half a day, he met a stranger.

The stranger stopped.

"Good day, boy," he said, "whither does God carry you ? "

And the boy said :

"I went to exchange the Easter greeting with my godmother ; when I came back home I asked my parents where my godfather lived, as I wanted to exchange the Easter greeting with him. My parents said to me : 'We do not know, son, where your godfather lives. After christening you, he went away from us, and we know nothing about him, and we do not know whether he is alive.' But I am anxious to see my godfather, and so I have started out to find him."

And the stranger said :

"I am your godfather."

The boy was happy, and exchanged the Easter greeting with his godfather.

"Whither are you, godfather, wending your way ? " he

asked. "If you are going in our direction, come to our house ; and if you are going home, I will go with you."

And the godfather said :

"I have no time to go now to your house, — I have some business in the villages. But I shall be at home to-morrow, so come to me then."

"But how shall I find you, father?"

"Walk all the time toward the rising of the sun, straight ahead, and you will come to a forest, and in the forest there is a clearing. Sit down in that clearing, rest yourself, and watch what will happen. When you come out of the forest, you will see a garden, and in the garden there is a booth with a golden roof : that is my house. Walk up to the gate, and I will come out to meet you."

Thus the godfather spoke, and disappeared from the godson's view.

IV.

The boy went as the godfather had told him. He walked and walked, and came to the forest. He came out on the clearing and saw in the middle of it a fir-tree, and on the fir-tree a rope was attached to a branch, and to the rope was tied an oak log weighing some three puds. Under the log there was a trough with honey.

The boy was wondering why the honey was placed there, and the log attached above it, when there was a crashing through the woods, and he saw bears coming out : in front was the she-bear ; she was followed by a yearling, and behind by three small cubs. The she-bear scented the air and went straight to the trough, and the cubs after her.

The she-bear stuck her muzzle into the honey : she called up the cubs, and they rushed up and made for the trough. The log moved away a little and turned back and struck the cubs. When the she-bear saw this, she moved the log away with her paw. The log moved

back farther, came back again, and struck into the midst
of the cubs, hitting some on the back and some on the
head.

The cubs howled and jumped away. The she-bear
grew furious, grabbed the log above her head with both
her paws, and swung it far away from herself. The log
flew up high; in the meantime the yearling ran up to the
trough, stuck his muzzle into the honey, and began to
lap it, and the others, too, began to come up to it. They
had barely come up, when the log swept back and
whacked the yearling on the head, killing him on the
spot. The she-bear growled more than ever, and grabbed
the log and sent it with all her strength flying upward.

The log flew higher than the branch, so that even the
rope was slackened, and the she-bear ran up to the
trough, and all the cubs with her. The log flew up and
up, and stopped, and started downward. The lower it
went, the faster it flew. It came down with a crash and
banged the she-bear on the head. She rolled over, jerked
her legs, and was dead. The cubs ran away.

v.

The boy marvelled at this, and walked on. He came
to a large garden, and in it there was a high palace with a
golden roof. The godfather was standing at the gate, and
smiling. He exchanged greetings with his godson, led
him through the gate, and took him through the garden.
Even in his dream the boy had not thought of such
beauty and joy as there were in this garden.

The godfather led the boy into the palace. The palace
was even more beautiful. He took the boy through all
the rooms: they were one more beautiful than the other,
and one more cheerful than the other, and he brought
him to a locked door.

"Do you see this door?" he said. "There is no lock

on it, — there are only some seals.   It is possible to open it, but I command you not to do so.   Live and enjoy yourself wherever and however you please ; enjoy all joys, but this is the one commandment : do not enter through this door.   But if you do go in through it, remember what you saw in the woods."

The godfather said this, and went away.   The godson was left alone, and began to live.   He was so happy and so cheerful that he thought he had lived here but three hours, whereas thirty years had passed.   When the thirty years had passed, the godson went up to the sealed door and thought :

" Why did my godfather not permit me to enter this room ?   I will go and see what there is there."

He pushed the door, the seals flew back, and the door opened.   The godson went in, and he saw larger and more beautiful rooms than any, and in the middle of the rooms stood a golden throne.   The godson walked from one room to another, and he went up to the throne, and walked up its steps and sat down.   Near the throne he saw a sceptre.   He took the sceptre into his hands.   The moment he lifted it, all four walls of the room disappeared, and he saw everything which was going on in the world.   He looked straight ahead of him, and he saw the sea, and ships sailing on it.   He looked to the right and he saw where foreign, non-Christian people were living.   He looked to the left, and he saw where Christian people, but not Russians, were living.   He looked into the fourth side, and there were our Russians.

" I will just see," he said, " what is going on at home, — whether the corn grows well there."

He looked at his field and saw cocks of corn there. He began to count the cocks, to see how much corn there was, and he saw a cart coming into the field, and a man sitting inside of it.   The godson thought that his father was coming in the night to haul away the ricks.

He took a good look at him, and saw that it was Váska Kudrashóv, the thief, who was coming in the cart. He drove up to the cocks, and began to load them on. That made the godson angry. He shouted:

"Father, your sheaves are being stolen from the field!"

His father woke up in the pasture.

"I had a dream that they are stealing my sheaves," he said. "I must go and see."

He jumped on a horse, and rode off. When he came to the field, he saw Vasíli, and so he called the peasants together. They beat Vasíli, and tied him, and took him to the jail.

The godson now looked into the town where his godmother was living. He saw her married to a merchant. She was lying and sleeping, but her husband got up and went to his mistress. The godson cried to his godmother:

"Get up! Your husband is doing something bad."

His godmother jumped up, dressed herself, found out where her husband was, disgraced and beat the mistress, and drove her husband away from her.

Then the godson looked at his mother, and saw her lying in the hut, and a robber slinking into the house and breaking into her trunk.

The mother awoke, and cried aloud. When the robber saw her, he took hold of an axe, and swung it, wishing to kill her.

The godson did not hold out, but hurled the sceptre at the robber, and struck him straight on his temple, and killed him on the spot.

VI

The moment the godson killed the robber, the walls closed up again, and the room became what it was.

The door opened, and the godfather came in. He

walked over to his godson, took his hand, led him down from the throne, and said:

"You did not obey my command, — you have done a bad thing in opening the forbidden door; another bad thing you did when you ascended the throne and took my sceptre; a third bad thing you did, — you added much evil to the world. If you had been sitting here another hour, you would have ruined half the people."

And the godfather led his godson up to the throne, and took the sceptre into his hand. And again were the walls removed, and everything became visible.

And the godfather said:

"See now what you have done to your father! Vasíli has been a year in prison, where he has learned all kinds of evil deeds and has become entirely a beast. See there! He has driven off two of your father's horses, and, you see, he is setting fire to his farmhouses. This is what you have done to your father."

The moment the godson saw his father's house on fire, the godfather hid this from him, and ordered him to look in another direction.

"Here," he said, "the husband of your godmother has abandoned his wife for more than a year, and is making free with other women, while she, from grief, has taken to drink, and his former mistress is entirely lost. This is what you have done to your godmother."

And the godfather hid this from him, and showed him his house. And he saw his mother: she was weeping on account of her sins, and repenting them, and saying, "It would have been better if the murderer had killed me then, for I should not have committed so many sins."

"This is what you have done to your mother."

And the godfather hid this, too, from him, and pointed downward. And the godson saw the robber: two guards were holding him before the dark place.

And the godfather said to him:

" This man has ruined nine souls. He ought to redeem his own sins; but you have killed him, and so have taken all his sins upon yourself. Now you will have to answer for all his sins. That is what you have done to yourself. The she-bear pushed away the log, and so disturbed the cubs; she pushed it away a second time, and killed the yearling; she pushed it away a third time, and killed herself. You have done the same. I give you now thirty years' time. Go into the world, and redeem the sins of the robber. If you do not redeem them, you will have to go in his place."

And the godson said :

" How can I redeem his sins ? "

And the godfather said :

" When you shall have freed the world from as much evil as you have carried into it, you will have redeemed your sins as well as those of the robber."

And the godson asked :

" How can I free the world from sins ? "

And the godfather said :

" Go straight toward the rising sun, and you will come to a field, with men upon it. Watch the people to see what they are doing, and teach them what you know. Then walk on, and take note of what you see; on the fourth day you will come to a forest; in the forest there is a cell, and in the cell lives a hermit. Tell him everything that has happened. He will teach you what to do. When you have done everything that the hermit commands you to do, you will have redeemed your sins and those of the robber."

Thus spoke the godfather, and he saw his godson out of the gate.

VII.

The godson went away. As he walked, he thought :

" How can I free the world from evil ? They destroy

evil by sending evil people to hard labour, locking them up in prisons, and putting them to death. What shall I do, then, to destroy evil, and not to take other people's sins upon myself?"

The godson thought and thought, but could not think out anything. He walked for a long time, and finally came to a field. In the field the corn had grown large and thick, and it was time to harvest it. The godson saw a heifer get into the corn. When the people saw it, they mounted their horses, and began to drive the heifer through the corn, now from one side and now from another. The moment the heifer was ready to run out of the corn, a rider passed by, which frightened the heifer, and she went back into the corn; again they galloped after her through the corn. But a woman was standing in the road, and weeping: "They are going to get my heifer."

And the godson said to the peasants:

"Why are you doing this? Ride all of you out of the corn. Let the woman call her heifer!"

The people obeyed him. The woman went up to the edge and began to call her heifer: "Tpryusi, tpryusi, browny, tpryusi, tpryusi!"

The heifer pricked her ears, stopped to listen, and ran straight toward the woman, and put her mouth into the woman's lap, almost knocking her down. And the peasants were glad, and the woman was glad, and the heifer was glad.

The godson walked on, thinking:

"Now I see that evil increases through evil. The more people persecute evil, the more do they multiply it. It is evident that evil cannot be destroyed through evil. But I do not know how to destroy it. It is well that the heifer obeyed her mistress; but how could she have been called out, if she had not obeyed?"

The godson thought and thought, but could not think it out. He went farther.

VIII.

He walked and walked, until he came to a village. He asked at the outer hut to be allowed to stay there overnight. The mistress let him in. There was no one in the hut but the mistress, and she was washing.

The godson went in, climbed on the oven, and began to look around, to see what the mistress was doing. He saw that she had washed the house, and was now washing the table. After she had washed the table, she began to wipe it with a dirty towel. She began to wipe it on one side, but the table did not get clean: the dirty towel left strips of dirt on the table. She began to wipe in another direction; she wiped off some of the stripes, but made other stripes come out. She began once more to rub lengthwise, and again it was the same: she soiled the table with the dirty towel. She wiped off the dirt in one place, and rubbed it on in another. The godson looked at it for awhile, and said:

"Mistress, what are you doing there?"

"Do you not see?" she said. "I am cleaning up for the holiday. I somehow cannot get the table clean, — it is so dirty. I am all worn out from it."

"If you would just wash the towel," he said, "you would be able to get it clean."

The mistress did so, and she got her table clean.

"Thank you," she said, "for having taught me."

Next morning the godson bade the mistress good-bye, and went away. He walked and walked, and came to a forest. There he saw some peasants bending hoops. The godson went up to them, and saw the peasants walking in a circle, but the hoop did not bend. He looked on awhile, and saw that the vise was not fastened, but turning around. So he said:

"Friends, what are you doing there?"

"We are bending hoops. We have steamed them twice, and we are all worn out, — they do not bend."

"Friends, fasten the vise, for you are turning around with it."

The peasants obeyed him, fastened the vise, and things went after that.

The godson remained with them overnight, and went farther. He walked a whole day and a night, and before the dawn came to some drovers. He lay down near them. He saw that the drovers had put away the cattle, and were trying to start a fire. They took dry leaves and set them on fire, and before they burned well, they put on them wet twigs. The twigs hissed, and the fire went out. The drovers took some more dry leaves and set them on fire, and again put on wet twigs. The fire was again put out. They worked for a long time, but the fire would not burn.

And the godson said:

"Don't be in a hurry to put on the twigs, but first let the leaves burn well. When the fire is well started, you may put on the twigs."

The drovers did so: they started a good fire, and then heaped up the twigs. The twigs caught fire and burned well. The godson remained with them awhile, and then went farther. He thought and thought why he had seen these three things, but he could not understand.

IX.

The godson walked and walked. A day passed. He came to a forest, and in the forest was a cell. He went up to the cell, and knocked. A voice inside asked:

"Who is there?"

"A great sinner: I want to redeem other people's sins."

The hermit came out, and asked:

"What are those sins of other people which are upon you?"

The godson told him everything: about his godfather, and about the she-bear and her cubs, and about the throne in the sealed room, and about what the godfather had commanded him to do, and about his having seen the peasants trample down all the corn, and about the heifer's coming out herself to her mistress.

"I now understand that evil cannot be destroyed by evil, but I cannot understand how it is to be destroyed. Teach me how."

And the hermit said:

"Tell me what else you saw on the road."

The godson told him about the woman's cleaning up, and about the peasants' bending of the hoops, and about the drovers' making a fire.

When the hermit had heard it all, he went back to his cell and brought out a notched and battered axe.

"Come with me," he said.

The hermit went a distance away from the cell, and pointed to a tree.

"Cut it down," he said.

The godson cut the tree, and it fell down.

"Cut it now into three parts."

The godson cut it into three parts. The hermit went again into the cell, and brought some fire.

"Burn the three logs," he said.

The godson started the fire and burned the three logs, and three smudges were left.

"Bury them half into the ground, — like this."

The godson buried them.

"You see, at the foot of the hill is a river: bring the water from there in your mouth, and water them. Water this smudge as you taught the woman; water this smudge as you taught the coopers; water this smudge as you taught the drovers. When all three shall have sprouted and three apple-trees shall have grown from the smudges, you will know how to destroy evil among men; and then you will redeem the sins."

Having said this, the hermit went back to his cell. The godson thought and thought, but could not understand what the hermit had told him. However, he did as he was commanded.

X.

The godson went to the river, filled his mouth full of water, poured it out on a smudge, and went back for more, — and so he watered the other two smudges. The godson grew tired, and wanted to eat. He went to the cell, to ask the hermit for something to eat. He opened the door, but the hermit lay dead on a bench. The godson looked around and found some hardtack, which he ate; then he found a spade, and began to dig a grave for the hermit. In the night he carried water to the smudges, and in the daytime he dug the grave. He had just finished the grave and was about to bury the hermit, when people came from the village, bringing food for the hermit.

The people learned that the hermit had died, and that he had blessed the godson in his place. The people buried the hermit, and left the bread for the godson; they promised to bring him more, and went away.

And so the godson remained to live in the place of the hermit. He lived there, and ate what the people brought to him, and kept doing the work which he had been commanded to do, carrying water in his mouth from the river, to water the smudges.

Thus the godson passed a year, and many people began to come to him. The rumour went abroad that a holy man was living in the forest, finding his salvation in carrying water in his mouth from the river at the foot of the hill, and watering the burned stumps. A multitude began to come to him.   Rich merchants, too, began to come to him, bringing him presents.   The godson took nothing from them, except what he needed, and what they gave him, he turned over to other poor people.

And this is the way the godson lived : half the day he carried water in his mouth, watering the smudges, and the other half he rested himself and received the people.

And the godson came to think that he had been commanded to live in this manner, thus destroying evil and redeeming sins.

So the godson lived another year, and did not miss watering the smudges a single day, but they did not sprout.

One day he was sitting in the cell, when he heard a man ride by him singing songs.   The godson went out to see who the man was.   He saw that he was a strong lad. He wore good clothes, and his horse and the saddle under him were fine.

The godson stopped him, and asked him what kind of a man he was and whither he was riding.

The man stopped.

" I am a robber," he said, " and am travelling along the roads, killing people : the more people I kill, the merrier the songs are which I sing."

The godson was frightened, and said :

" How can I destroy the evil in this man ?   It is easy enough for me to talk to those who come to me, and themselves repent their sins.   But this one boasts of evil."

The godson did not say anything, but went away, and thought what to do now.   " If the robber takes it into his head to rove here, the people will become scared, and will stop coming to see me.   They will lose their advantage, and how shall I live then ? "

And the godson stopped, and said to the robber:

"People come here, not to boast of evil, but to repent and to pray for their sins. Repent, if you are afraid of God; if you do not wish to repent, go away from here, and never come back to disturb me, and to frighten the people. If you will not pay any attention to me, God will punish you."

The robber laughed.

"I am not afraid of God," he said, "and I will pay no attention to you. You are not my master. You live by your praying, and I live by robbery. All have to live in some way. Teach the women that come to see you, but you cannot teach me. Since you have mentioned God to me, I will kill two additional men to-morrow. I should have killed you, but I do not want to soil my hands. Don't ever get in my way again."

Thus the robber threatened him, and went away. He never came back, and the godson lived quietly, as before, for eight years.

XI.

One night the godson went out to water his smudges. He came back to the cell, to rest himself, and he sat and looked at the footpath, to see whether people would come soon. On that day not one man came. The godson sat there alone until evening, and he felt lonely, and thought about his life. He remembered how the robber had rebuked him for living by praying. And so the godson looked back upon his life.

"I am not living as the hermit told me to," he thought. "The hermit imposed a penance on me, while I have earned a living and fame by it. And I have been so tempted by it that I feel lonely when people do not come to me. I have not redeemed my former sins, and have only added new ones. I will go into the woods, to another place, so that the people may not find me. I will live all by myself, so as to redeem my old sins, and not add new ones."

Thus thought the hermit, and he took a bag full of hardtack and a spade, and went away from the cell, toward a ravine, in order to build him an earth hut in a hidden place, where the people might not see him.

The godson was walking with his bag and with his spade, when the robber rode up to him. The godson became frightened, and wanted to run, but the robber overtook him.

"Whither are you going?" he said.

The godson told him that he wanted to go away from the people, to a place where the people could not reach him. The robber was surprised.

"What will you now live by, if people stop coming to you?"

The godson had not thought of it before, but when the robber asked him this, he thought of the food.

"By what God will give me," he said.

The robber said nothing, and rode on.

"Why did I not tell him anything about his life?" thought the godson. "Maybe he would repent now. He seems to be kinder to-day, and did not threaten to kill me."

And the godson called out to the robber:

"But still you must repent. You cannot get away from God."

The robber turned his horse around. He pulled his knife out of the girdle, and swung it to strike the godson. The godson became frightened, and ran into the forest.

The robber did not run after him, but only said:

"Twice have I forgiven you, but if you come in my way the third time, I will kill you."

Having said this, he rode off. In the evening the godson went to water the smudges, and, behold, one of them had sprouted; an apple-tree was growing from it.

XII.

The godson hid himself from the people, and began to live alone. His hardtack gave out.

" Well," he thought, " now I will look for herbs."

He went out to look for herbs, when he saw a bag with hardtack hanging on a branch. He took it, and lived on that hardtack.

When this hardtack gave out, another bag of it was hanging on the same branch. And thus the godson lived. But he had this grief, — he was afraid of the robber. Whenever he heard the robber, he hid himself. He thought:

" If he kills me, I shall not have a chance to redeem my sins."

Thus he lived another ten years. The one apple-tree grew, but the other smudges remained such as they were.

One morning the godson went early to do his work; he watered the earth around the smudges, and he was tired and sat down to rest himself. He was sitting and resting himself, and thinking:

" I have sinned, to be afraid of death. If God so wishes, I can redeem my sins by my death."

No sooner had he said this, than he heard the robber riding along, and cursing. The godson heard him, and thought:

" Except from God, nothing good nor evil will befall me from anybody," and he went to meet the robber.

He saw that the robber was not travelling by himself, but was bringing a man with him on the saddle. The man's hands and mouth were tied. The man was silent, and the robber kept cursing him. The godson went up to the robber, and stood in front of the horse.

" Whither are you taking this man?" he asked.

" I am taking him to the forest. He is the son of a

merchant. He will not tell me where his father's money is hidden, and I will flog him until he does tell."

The robber wanted to ride on ; but the godson did not let him, — he seized the horse by the bridle.

" Let this man go," he said.

The robber grew angry at the godson, and wanted to strike him.

" Do you want me to do the same to you ? I have told you I would kill you. Let me go ! "

The godson was not frightened.

" I will not let you go," he said. " I am not afraid of you, but only of God. God does not allow me let you go. Set the man free ! "

The robber scowled, took out his knife, cut the ropes, and set free the merchant's son.

" Get away from me," he said. " Let me not catch you again ! "

The merchant's son leaped down and ran away. The robber wanted to ride on, but the godson stopped him again ; he began to talk to him about giving up his bad life. The robber stood still awhile and listened to all he had to say, but said nothing, and rode off.

The next morning the godson went to water the smudges. Behold, another smudge had sprouted, — again it was an apple-tree that was growing from it.

XIII.

Another ten years passed. One day the godson was sitting. He was not wishing for anything, and he was not afraid of anything, and his heart was glad. And the godson thought :

" What grace is given by God to men ! But they torment themselves in vain. They ought to live in joy all the time."

And he thought of all the evil of men, and how they

tormented themselves. And he began to feel sorry for men.

"In vain," he thought, "I live this way; I must go and tell people what I know."

No sooner had he thought so, than he heard the robber coming along. He let the robber pass by him, and thought:

"What use is there in speaking to him? He will not understand."

At first he thought so, but he thought it over again, and went out on the road. The robber passed by, looking gloomy and staring at the ground. The godson looked at him, and felt sorry for him, and ran up to him, and seized him by his knee.

"Dear brother," he said, "have pity on thy soul! God's spirit is in you! You are suffering yourself, and are causing others to suffer, and you will suffer even more. But God loves you, and has such grace in store for you! Do not ruin yourself, brother! Change your life!"

The robber scowled, and turned his face away.

"Get away from me," he said.

The godson embraced the robber's knee even more firmly and began to weep.

The robber raised his eyes to the godson. He looked and looked at him, and climbed down from his horse, and knelt before the godson.

"You have vanquished me, old man," he said. "Twenty years have I struggled with you, and you have overcome me. I have no power over myself; you can do with me what you please. When you tried to persuade me the first time, I only grew more savage. I began to think of your speeches only when you went away from people and found out that you yourself did not need anything from men."

And the godson recalled that the woman washed the table clean only when she washed the towel. When he stopped caring for himself, and cleansed his own heart, he was able to cleanse also the hearts of others.

And the robber said:

"And my heart turned in me only when you did not fear death."

And the godson recalled that the coopers could bend the hoop only when the vise was made firm. When he stopped fearing death, and made his life firm in God, the unruly heart was vanquished.

And the robber said:

"And my heart melted completely only when you took pity on me and wept before me."

The godson was happy, and led the robber to where the smudges were. When they came up to them, an apple-tree had sprouted from the third smudge. And the godson recalled that the wet branches caught fire with the drovers only when the fire burned bright. When his heart burned bright, another man's heart, too, burned up.

And the godson was glad, because now he had redeemed the sins.

He told all this to the robber, and died. The robber buried him, and began to live as the godson had commanded him, and so he taught the people.

THREE SONS
1892

THREE SONS

———◆———

A FATHER gave his son some property, corn, and cattle, and said to him:

"Live like me, and thou wilt always fare well."

The son took his patrimony, went away from the father, and began to live for his pleasure. The father had, indeed, told him to live like him. "He lives and enjoys himself, and so will I."

Thus he lived a year, two, ten, twenty years, — and wasted all his patrimony, and he had nothing left; and he began to ask his father to give him more; but his father did not listen to him. Then he began to propitiate his father and to give to him the best things he had, and to ask him again. But his father made no reply to him. Then the son began to ask his father's forgiveness, thinking that he had offended him in some way, and again asked him to give him something; but his father did not say a word.

Then the son began to imprecate his father, saying:

"If thou dost not give me now, why didst thou give me before and dole out my part to me and promise me that I should fare well? All my former joys, when I spent my estate, are not worth one hour of the present torments. I see that I perish, and there is no salvation. And who is to blame? Thou. Thou knewest that my estate would not be sufficient, and thou didst not give me more. All thou toldest me was, "Live like me, and thou wilt fare well. And I lived like thee. Thou livedst for thy joy, and I lived for mine. Thou hast more left for thyself, so thou hast some, while I have not enough. Thou art not a father, but a deceiver and evil-doer! Cursed is my life, and cursed be thou, evil-doer and tormentor, — I do not want to know thee, and I hate thee!"

The father gave also some property to the second son, saying only:

" Live like me, and thou wilt always fare well."

The second son was not so much rejoiced at his estate as had been the first. He thought that he received his due; but he knew what had happened with his elder brother, and so began to think that he might lose his property like the first. He understood this much, that his eldest brother had not understood correctly the words, " Live like me," and that it was not right to live only for one's own pleasure.

He began to brood over the words, " Live like me."

And he reasoned out that it was necessary, as his father had done, to put to profit the estate which his father gave him. And he began to ask his father how to do this or that, but his father made no reply to him. Then the son thought that his father was afraid to tell him, and began to take to pieces all his father's things, in order to see for himself how everything was done, and he spoiled and ruined everything which he had received from his father, and everything new which he did was all to no profit. But he did not want to acknowledge that he had spoiled everything, and so he lived in agony, telling all that his father had given him nothing, but that he had made everything for himself. " We can all of us do better and better, and shall soon reach a point when everything will be well." Thus spoke the second son, so long as anything his father had given him was left with him; but when he had spent the last, and he had nothing to live on, he laid hands on himself and killed himself.

The father gave just such an estate to the third son, and told him too:

" Live like me, and then thou wilt always fare well."

And the third son, like the first and the second, was glad to receive the estate, and went away from his father; but he knew what had happened with his elder brothers and began to think of what was meant by the words, " Live like me, and thou wilt always prosper."

The eldest brother had thought that to live like the father meant to live for his own pleasure, and he squandered everything, and was ruined.

The second brother had thought that to live like his father meant for him to do everything which his father had done, and he, too, came to despair. What, then, is meant by living like the father ?

And he began to recall everything he knew about his father. And no matter how much he thought, he could not think of anything else about his father except that formerly there had been nothing, not even himself, and that his father had begotten, brought up, and educated him, and had taught and given him everything good, and had said, " Live like me, and thou wilt always prosper." Even thus his father had done with his brothers. And no matter how much he thought, he could not think of anything else about his father, except that his father had done good to him and to his brothers.

And then he comprehended what these words meant. He understood that to live like the father meant to do what he was doing, to do good to men. And when he thought of this, his father was already near him, and said :

" Here we are again together, and thou wilt always fare well. Go to thy brother and to all of my children, and tell them what is meant by, ' Live like me,' and that those who will live like me will always fare well."

And the third son went and told everything to his

brother, and since then all the children, in receiving their estate from their father, have not rejoiced because they have a large estate, but because they can live like the father, and will always fare well.

The father is God; His sons are men; the estate is life. Men think that they can live alone without God.

Some of these men think that their life is given to them in order to rejoice in this life. They rejoice and waste this life, and when the time comes to die, they do not understand why such life was given to them, since its joys end in suffering and death. And these men die, cursing God and calling Him evil, and depart from God.

This is the first son.

Other men think that life is given to them in order that they may understand how it is made, and in order that they may make it better than what is given them by God. And they struggle over it, to make another, a better life. But, in improving this life, they ruin it, and thus deprive themselves of life.

Other people say:

" Everything we know of God is that He gives the good to men and commands them to do the same, and so let us do the same that He does, — good to men."

And the moment they begin to do so, God Himself comes to them, and says:

" This is precisely what I wanted. Do with me what I do, and as I live, so shall you live."

LABOURER EMELYAN AND THE EMPTY DRUM

A Fairy-Tale

1892

LABOURER EMELYÁN AND THE EMPTY DRUM[1]

EMELYÁN was working for a master. One day he was walking over the field, to his work, when a frog jumped up before him: he almost stepped on it. Emelyán stepped over it. Suddenly he heard some one calling him from behind. He looked around, and saw there standing a beautiful maiden, and she said to him:

"Emelyán, why do you not get married?"

"How can I marry, pretty maid? All I have is what I carry with me, and no one will have me."

And the maiden said:

"Take me for a wife!"

Emelyán took a liking to the maiden.

"I would gladly marry you," he said, "but where shall we live?"

"We shall think of that," said the maiden. "If only we work much and sleep little, we shall be clothed and fed anywhere."

"Very well," he said, "let us get married! Whither shall we go?"

"Let us go to the city."

Emelyán went with the maiden to the city. She took him to a small house at the edge of the city, and they were married, and began to live.

[1] A popular tale, created along the Vólga in the remote past, and reconstructed by Tolstóy.

One day the king drove beyond the city. As he passed by Emelyán's house, his wife came out to look at the king. The king saw her, and marvelled:

"Where was such a beauty born?"

The king stopped his carriage, and called up Emelyán's wife, and began to ask her:

"Who are you?"

"I am the wife of Peasant Emelyán," she said.

"Why have you, who are such a beauty, married a peasant?" he said. "You ought to be a queen."

"I thank you for your kind words," she said. "I am satisfied with a peasant."

The king spoke with her, and drove on. He returned to his palace. He could not forget Emelyán's wife. He could not sleep the whole night long, thinking all the time how he might take Emelyán's wife away. He could not think how it could be done. He called his servants, and commanded them to think it out. And the servants of the king said to him:

"Take Emelyán into your palace to work for you. We will kill him with work, and his wife will be left a widow, then you can take her."

So the king did: he sent for Emelyán, commanding him to be a janitor in his palace, and to live in the palace with his wife.

The messengers went to Emelyán, and told him so. His wife said:

"Why not? Go! Work in the daytime, and come to me in the night!"

Emelyán went. When he came to the palace, the king's steward asked him:

"Why did you come by yourself, without your wife?"

"Why should I bring her? She has a house of her own."

They gave Emelyán work enough for two to do. Emelyán took hold of the work, thinking he would never finish it; but, behold, he finished it before night. When the steward saw that he got through with it, he gave him for the next day enough for four to do. Emelyán went home; but at his home everything was swept clean and tidied: the fire was made in the oven, and everything was baked and cooled. His wife was sitting at the table, sewing at something, and waiting for her husband. She met her husband, got the supper ready, gave him to eat and to drink, and began to ask him about his work.

"Things are bad," he said. "They give me tasks beyond my strength: they will kill me with work."

"Do not think of work," she said. "Look neither forward nor backward, whether you have done much, or whether much is left to do. Work, and everything will come out in proper time."

Emelyán lay down to sleep. In the morning he went out again. He took hold of the work, and did not look back once. Behold, in the evening everything was done, and he went home to sleep, while it was yet light. They kept increasing his task, but he finished his work in time, and went home to sleep.

A week passed. The king's servants saw that they could not wear out Emelyán with hard labour, and so began to give him cunning tasks; but they could not wear him out with these, either. No matter what they gave him to do, whether carpenter's, or mason's, or thatcher's work, he finished all by the set time, and went home to his wife to sleep. Another week passed. The king called up his servants, and said to them:

"Do I feed you for nothing? Two weeks have passed, and I do not see anything from you. You were going to kill Emelyán with work, and I see each day through the window that he goes home singing songs. Do you mean to make fun of me?"

The king's servants began to justify themselves.

"We have tried with all our might and main to wear

him out, first of all, with menial labour, but we could not vanquish him. No matter what we gave him to do, he did, as though sweeping it clean, and feeling no weariness. We began to give him cunning work to do, thinking that he would not have sense enough, and still we could not overcome him. Where does it all come from? He understands everything, and does everything. Either there is some witchery in him, or in his wife. We are ourselves tired of him. We want to give him now such work to do that he will be unable to finish it. We have decided to ask him to build a cathedral in one day. Call in Emelyán, and command him in one day to build a cathedral opposite the palace. And if he does not build it, we can chop off his head for his disobedience."

The king sent for Emelyán.

"Here is my command," he said: "Build me a new cathedral opposite the palace, on the square. It has to be ready by to-morrow evening. If you get it built, I shall reward you; but if you do not, I shall put you to death."

When Emelyán had heard the king's words, he turned around and went home.

"Well," he thought, "now my end has come."

He came to his wife and said:

"Wife, get ready! you must run away wherever you can, or else you will lose your life."

"What frightens you so," she said, "that you want to run?"

"How can I help being frightened? The king has commanded me to build a cathedral to-morrow, in one day. If I do not get it built, he threatens to chop off my head. There is nothing left to do but run away."

His wife did not accept his words.

"The king has many soldiers, and he will catch you anywhere. You cannot run away from him. So long as you have strength you must obey him."

"But how shall I obey, if I have not the strength?"

"Never mind, husband. Do not trouble yourself: eat your supper and lie down to sleep; get up early in the morning, and all will go well."

Emelyán lay down to sleep; his wife woke him up.

"Go," she said, "and finish the cathedral as quickly as you can. Here are nails and a hammer. You will find about a day's work left to do."

Emelyán went into the city, and there, indeed, the cathedral was standing in the middle of the square, just a little unfinished. Emelyán began to put on the last touches, wherever necessary, and by evening he had everything done. The king woke up, looked out of the palace, and, behold, there was the cathedral, and Emelyán was walking to and fro, driving in nails here and there. The king was not at all pleased with the cathedral: he was angry, because he had no reason to put him to death, and could not take his wife from him. The king again called his servants.

"Emelyán has done this task, too, and I have no cause to kill him. This task was not big enough for him. You must invent something more cunning. Think out something, or else I will have you put to death before him."

The servants thought out to have Emelyán construct a river around the palace, so that ships might sail on it. The king called Emelyán, and commanded him to do a new task.

"If you were able to build a cathedral in one night," he said, "you are also able to do this work: everything is to be ready by to-morrow as I command. If it is not ready, I shall have your head cut off."

Emelyán was grieved more than ever, and came home gloomy to his wife.

"Why are you so sad? Has the king commanded you to do something new?"

Emelyán told her.

"We must run away."

But his wife said:

"You cannot run away from the soldiers, — they will catch you anywhere. You must obey."

"But how can I obey?"

"Come now, come now, husband, do not worry! Eat your supper, and lie down to sleep. Get up as early as possible, and all will be in good time."

Emelyán lay down to sleep. His wife woke him up in the morning.

"Go to the castle," she said. "Everything is ready. Near the harbour, opposite the palace, a little mound is left: so take a spade and even it up."

Emelyán went. When he came to the city he saw a river round about the palace, and the ships were sailing upon it. Emelyán went up to the harbour, opposite the palace, and he saw an uneven place, and evened it up.

The king awoke, and he saw a river where there had been none before; ships were sailing on the river, and Emelyán was evening up a mound with a spade. The king was frightened and not at all glad of the river and the ships, but annoyed, because he could not put Emelyán to death. He thought to himself: "There is no task which he cannot do. What shall I do?" He called up his servants and took counsel with them.

"Think out a task," he said, "which will be beyond Emelyán; for so far, no matter what we have given him to do, he has done, and I am not able to get his wife from him."

The courtiers thought and thought, and finally thought out something. They came to the king and said:

"Emelyán ought to be called and told this: 'Go there, know not where, and bring that, know not what!' He will not be able to get away this time, for wherever he may go, you will say that he did not go where it was necessary, and no matter what he may bring, you will say

that he did not bring the right thing. Then you can put
him to death and take his wife."

The king was happy.

"This is a clever thought of yours," he said.

The king sent for Emelyán, and said to him:

"Go there, know not where, bring that, know not
what. If you do not bring it, I shall have your head
cut off."

Emelyán came to his wife, and told her what the king
had said to him. The wife thought awhile.

"Well," she said, "they have instructed the king
cleverly. Now we must do it well."

His wife sat awhile thinking, and then she said to her
husband:

"You will have to go a long distance, — to our grandmother, the ancient peasant, soldier mother, — and you
must ask her favour. If you get anything from her, go
straight to the palace, and I will be there. Now I cannot
get out of their hands. They will take me by force, but
it will not be for long. If you do everything as the
grandmother tells you to, you will redeem me soon."

The wife got her husband ready, and gave him a wallet
and a spindle.

"Give this to her," she said. "By this will she tell
that you are my husband."

She showed him the road. Emelyán went away.
When he came outside the city, he saw them teaching
the soldiers. He stood still for awhile, watching them.
After the soldiers had practised, they sat down to rest
themselves. Emelyán went up to them, and asked:

"Brothers, can you tell me how to go there, know not
where, and how to bring that, know not what?"

When the soldiers heard this, they marvelled.

"Who sent you to find that?" they asked.

"The king," he said.

"We ourselves," they said, "ever since we have been

made soldiers, have been going there, know not where, and cannot get there, and have been seeking that, know not what, and cannot find it. We cannot help you."

Emelyán sat awhile with the soldiers, and went on. He walked and walked, and came to a forest. In the forest there was a hut. In the hut sat an old woman, — the peasant, soldier mother, — spinning at the wheel. She was weeping and did not moisten her fingers with her spittle in her mouth, but with the tears in her eyes. When the old woman saw Emelyán, she called out to him:

" What did you come here for ? "

Emelyán gave her the spindle, and said that his wife had sent him to her. The old woman softened at once, and began to put questions to him. And Emelyán told her all about his life, how he had married the maiden; how he had gone to the city to live; how he had been made a janitor; how he had served in the palace; how he had built the cathedral and had made a river with its ships, and how the king had commanded him to go there, know not where, and bring that, know not what.

The old woman listened to him and stopped weeping. She began to mumble to herself:

" The time has evidently come. Very well," she said, " sit down, my son, and have something to eat."

Emelyán had something to eat, and the old woman said to him:

" Here you have a ball of twine: roll it before you, and follow it, wherever it rolls. It will roll far away, to the very sea. You will come to the sea, and there you will see a large city. Go into the city, and ask them in the outer house to let you stay there overnight. Then look for what you need ! "

" How shall I know it, grandmother ? "

" When you see that which people obey better than their parents, you have found it. Grasp it and take it to the king! When you bring it to the king, he will say to you that you have not brought the right thing; say then, 'If it is not that I shall have to break it,' and strike the thing and then take it to the river, break it to pieces, and throw it into the water; then you will get your wife back, and you will dry up my tears."

Emelyán bade the old woman good-bye, and went away, rolling the ball before him. He rolled it and rolled it, and it brought him to the sea. Near the sea was a large city. At the edge of it stood a large house. Emelyán asked the people in the house to let him stay in it overnight, and they let him. He lay down to sleep. He woke up early in the morning, and heard the father getting up and waking his son, to send him to cut some wood. And the son did not obey him:

"It is early yet: I shall have time enough to do it."

He heard the mother say on the oven:

"Go, my son, your father's bones are aching, — how can he go himself? It is time."

The son only smacked his lips, and fell asleep again. The moment he fell asleep, there was a thundering and rattling in the street. The son jumped up, dressed himself, and ran out into the street. Emelyán, too, jumped up and ran after him, to see what it was that the son paid more attention to than to his father and his mother. Emelyán ran out, and saw a man walking in the street, carrying a round thing over his belly, and striking it with sticks, and it was this that thundered so and made the son pay attention to it. Emelyán ran up to take a look at the thing. He saw that it was as round as a vat, and skins were stretched over both sides of it. He asked the people what they called this thing.

"A drum," they said.

"Is it empty?"

"Yes," they said.

Emelyán wondered at the thing, and began to ask the

man to give it to him. The man would not give it to him. Emelyán stopped asking for it, but followed the drummer. He walked the whole day, and when the drummer lay down to sleep, Emelyán seized the drum, and ran away with it. He ran and ran and came home to his city. He went to see his wife, but she was not at home. She had been taken to the king the next day. Emelyán went to the palace, and had himself announced.

" The man has come," he said, " who went there, know not where, and has brought that, know not what."

He was announced to the king. The king sent word to Emelyán to come the next day. Emelyán asked to be announced once more :

" I have come this day, and have brought what the king has commanded. Let the king come to me, or else will I go in myself."

The king came out.

" Where have you been ? " he asked.

He told him where.

" It is not there," he said. " And what did you bring ? "

Emelyán wanted to show it to him, but the king did not look at it.

" It is not that," he said.

" If it is not that," he said, " I must break it, and the devil take it ! "

Emelyán went out of the palace with the drum, and struck it. The moment he struck it, the whole army of the king gathered about Emelyán. They did not obey the king, but followed after Emelyán. When the king saw this, he ordered Emelyán's wife brought out to Emelyán, and began to ask him to give him the drum.

" I cannot," said Emelyán. " I have been commanded to break it to pieces, and to throw the pieces into the river."

Emelyán went with the drum to the river, and the

soldiers came after him. At the river, Emelyán broke the drum and smashed it to splinters, and threw them into the river. And all the soldiers ran away. But Emelyán took his wife and went home with her. After that the king stopped harassing him, and he began to live happily, gaining what was good, and losing what was evil.